Loons

Loons

Patrick Merrick

THE CHILD'S WORLD®, INC.

Library of Congress Cataloging-in-Publication Data
Merrick, Patrick.
Loons / by Patrick Merrick.
p.   cm.
Includes index.
Summary: Describes the physical characteristics,
behavior, habitat, and life cycle of loons.
ISBN 1-56766-595-0 (lib. bdg. : alk paper)
1. Loons—Juvenile literature.
[1. Loons.]   I. Title.
QL696.G33M46   1999
598.4′42—dc21   98-38203
CIP
AC

Photo Credits

ANIMALS ANIMALS © Alan G. Nelson: 19
ANIMALS ANIMALS © Tom Lazar: 24
© 1997 Carl R. Sams II/Dembinsky Photo Assoc. Inc.: 16
© Carl R. Sams II & Jean F. Stoick/Dembinsky Photo Assoc. Inc.: 6
© Daniel J. Cox/Natural Exposures, Inc.: 10, 13, 15, 30
© 1997 Jim Roetzel/Dembinsky Photo Assoc. Inc.: 9
© Richard R. Hansen, The National Audubon Society Collection/Photo Researchers: 29
© Stephen J. Krasemann, The National Audubon Society Collection/Photo Researchers: 20
© Stephen Kirkpatrick: 23, 26
© T. J. Ulrich/VIREO: 2
© Tom and Pat Leeson: cover

On the cover...

Front cover: This *common loon* is watching for danger as it sits on its nest.
Page 2: This beautiful common loon has made its nest in some tall grasses.

Table of Contents

As the sun begins to set over your campground, the only sounds you hear are the wind and the chirping of crickets. Soon, however, a strange sound rings out through the trees. It sounds like a crazy laugh—"Wha-Ha-Ha-Ha-Ha-Woooooo." What could be making that noise? You rush to the water's edge, but the only thing on the lake is a pretty black and white bird. When you look closer, you realize that it's the bird that is making that sound! What type of creature is it? It's a loon.

← This common loon and its chick are swimming slowly in a lake.

What Do Loons Look Like?

Loons are one of the oldest families of birds. They have been around for almost 60 million years! There are several different types, or **species,** of loons. Each species looks a little different. The *red-throated loon* has a patch of red color on the front of its neck. The *Pacific loon* has a gray head and white stripes. The best-known loon is the *common loon.* Common Loons are black and white. They have a smooth black head and a white band around their neck. All loons have deep red eyes and very pointed beaks.

This *Pacific loon* is sitting on its nest. ⇒

Loons are big birds. They can be over two and a half feet long and weigh over 15 pounds. Their **wingspan**—the distance from one wingtip to the other—is almost five feet! Loons have very large, powerful webbed feet. The feet are far back on the loon's body. That makes it hard for loons to walk. They stumble, and sometimes they fall to the ground and push along on their bellies.

← It is easy to see that this common loon has a big wingspan.

Where Do Loons Live?

Loons weren't made for walking—they were made for swimming. In fact, they spend most of their lives in the water. Once in the water, they are very graceful. In the spring and summer, loons live on lakes and rivers in northern Europe and Asia, Canada, and the northern United States. Loons are so popular that they are the official bird of Minnesota and the Canadian province of Ontario.

This common loon lives on a lake in northern Minnesota. ⇒

As the weather turns colder, most loons **migrate,** or travel south for the winter. Some loons stay on the northern oceans, which do not freeze. Most loons, however, head south before the lakes freeze. They fly to warmer places like California, Louisiana, or Florida. Loons migrate back and forth each year for their entire lives—up to 25 years.

Loons are strong, fast fliers. In fact, they can reach air speeds of over 100 miles an hour! But even though they are good fliers, they have a lot of trouble getting in the air. Most birds have hollow, light bones to help them fly. But a loon's bones are much more solid and heavy. The loon's heaviness means that it cannot take off like other birds. First it flaps its wings until most of its body is out of the water. Then it runs on top of the water! It needs to run for about 1,300 feet to get enough speed to take off.

⇐ This common loon is splashing a lot of water as it takes off.

What Do Loons Eat?

Loons are **predators,** which means that they are hunters that eat other animals. They eat small fish, insects, crayfish, frogs, and almost anything else that lives in the water. Loons are well **adapted,** or suited, to hunting in the water. Their sleek bodies can turn under the water quickly, and they can swim as fast as most fish! Loons are also excellent divers. They can dive over 200 feet deep and stay under water for more than five minutes!

This common loon is diving to look for food. ⇒

How Are Baby Loons Born?

Each pair of loons establishes a **territory,** or a home area, on a small lake or part of a larger lake. In the spring, the loons mate and find a place near shore where they can build a nest. Once they find a good nesting place, they come back to the same spot every year. After they build their nest, the female lays two eggs. Both the male and the female take turns sitting on the eggs and protecting them from enemies. The loons guard the eggs constantly. After about a month, the eggs finally hatch.

⇐ This *red-throated loon* is sitting on its nest in Alaska.

Are Loons Good Parents?

Baby loons, called **chicks,** have soft, dark brown feathers. When they are just a few hours old, the chicks are ready to take their first swim! Loons are very good parents. They teach their chicks how to swim and dive. If a baby gets tired, the parent lets it climb onto its back for a ride.

For the first few weeks, the parents bring the chicks food. After the babies are older, the parents teach them how to find their own food. By autumn, the chicks are almost fully grown. They are ready to migrate south for the winter.

These common loon chicks are riding on their parent's back. ⇒

Because they are such good swimmers, adult loons are safe from almost all enemies in the water. If they are on land, however, they are clumsy enough to be caught by lynx, foxes, or mink. For that reason, loons do not venture far from the water.

The most dangerous time for a loon is when it is very young. Many animals like to eat loon eggs. Raccoons, for example, have even eaten enough eggs to destroy most of a state's loon population! Once the chick hatches, life is no easier. Eagles and many other birds prey on the baby loons. Even the water isn't safe. Large fish such as muskie and northern pike come to the surface and swallow little chicks whole!

⇐ This common loon chick is only 3 weeks old.

Are Loons in Danger?

Loons have one other enemy—people. Every year, boaters and campers destroy many loon nests and **habitats,** or the types of areas in which loons live. Oil spills and other forms of pollution have killed many more loons. Some lakes have become so polluted that fish cannot live there and the loons cannot find enough to eat. Because of these problems, the number of loons has dropped by more than half.

This red-throated loon is covered with oil from a nearby spill. ⇒

To help the loons survive, we all need to be careful when we camp, fish, and boat. We also need to work to reduce pollution. If we do this, the strange and wonderful voice of the loon will sing for many summer nights to come.

⇐ This common loon is sitting on its nest near a Minnesota lake.

Glossary

adapted (uh–DAP–ted)
When an animal is well adapted, it is well suited to a certain way of life. Loons are well adapted to hunting and living in the water.

chicks (CHIKS)
Chicks are young birds. Loon chicks can swim even when they are very young.

habitats (HA–bih–tats)
A habitat is the type of area where an animal lives. A habitat includes the land, water, plants, and special items that make up the area.

migrate (MY–grate)
To migrate is to move back and forth from one place to another. Loons migrate to warmer southern waters each winter.

predators (PREH–duh–ter)
Predators are animals that hunt and kill other animals for food. Loons are predators that eat fish, frogs, insects, and other small water animals.

species (SPEE–sheez)
A species is a particular type of an animal. There are several different species of loons.

territory (TARE–ih–tor–ee)
A territory is an area of land that an animal claims as its own. Each pair of loons claims a lake area as its territory.

wingspan (WING–span)
A wingspan is the distance across a bird's wings, from one wingtip to the other. Loons have a wingspan of almost five feet.

Index